CUPID

is a

CNT

DREA DENAE

Cover Design by: Nikki Epperson

Published by: Drea Denae via Amazon Kindle Direct Publishing

Content Editing: Samantha Bee

❋ Created with Vellum

This one is for the Unholy Trinity.

Tottie and Stabby, you always make me feel like I'm enough. You don't kick me out of the group chat when I joke about snake peens. You told me to go for it when I had a half ass idea about a funny Valentine's Day themed novella.

I love you both so much.

A Note From The Author

Cupid is a C*nt is a Valentine's Day themed reverse harem novella.

This means it is intentionally a quick read with a little bit of plot and some steamy situations. I repeat, it is not a full-length book. Reverse harem means that the leading lady doesn't choose by the end of the story.

Please be mindful that this story may not be for you. If you choose to continue reading, you'll be thrown into a world of ridiculousness including puns and kinks.

Have fun.

CUPID'S

Extended Playlist
Available on Spotify

BOOM CLAP- CHARLI XCX

SECRET LOVE SONG- LITTLE MIX

SHE LOOKS SO PERFECT- 5 SECONDS OF SUMMER

SWEET TALK- SAMANTHA JADE

I SHOT CUPID- STELLA COLE

ROSES- THE CHAINSMOKERS, ROZES

OUT OF MY LEAGUE- FITZ AND THE TANTRUMS

PLAYLIST

CERTAIN THINGS- JAMES ARTHUR, CHASING GRACE

DISSOLVE- ABSOFACTO

NOTHING- BRUNO MAJOR

LOST IN THE FIRE- GESAFFELSTEIN, THE WEEKND

WANNA BE IN LOVE- LAUREN MARTINEZ

MAKE YOU MINE- PUBLIC

TITLE- MEGHAN TRAINOR

INTO YOUR ARMS- WITT LOWRY, AVA MAX

BEST IS YET TO COME- GRYFFIN, KYLE REYNOLDS

Chapter One

Val

"When have I ever steered you wrong, Val?"

I could name at least three times in the last year that my best friend Noel has gotten me involved in one of her ludicrous messes. It's like her superpower to find trouble. The girl could stir up a commotion in the calmest yoga studio and then look confused when someone has the audacity to be upset with her for it. It doesn't help that all she has to do is give me her signature pout and I'll do everything in my power to fix whatever has gone wrong.

She hooked up with a married couple in a bar bathroom one time just to have the wife steal her dress off the floor after. I marched into that stall, stripped off my shirt and tossed it over her head. Neither of us were ready to head home so I pretended my bra was a risqué crop top, while Noel is short enough that my top was just an extra short mini dress on her.

There was the time she told me that the park was hosting an open mic night and she wanted to go and watch the cute guy from the coffee shop who was supposed to be performing. When we showed up, it was him and a karaoke machine. He used the microphone to beat a heckler within an inch of his life before raking his hand through his boy band hair and asking if we were a two for one deal.

Or last week when she said she planned a blind double date for us, but instead she tricked the same married couple from scenario number one into meeting her for a repeat. Her plan was apparently for both of us to seduce them, get into their home and I was going to steal the dress while she distracted them. Except the wife showed up wearing Noel's dress. I had to drag my friend out of the restaurant because she attempted to tear it off her in a fit of rage.

"Valley girl, are you listening to me?" I am the opposite of a valley girl, but Noel's nicknames aren't designed to make sense to anyone but her.

Rolling my eyes, I get off the couch and make my way to the coffee. "I'm sorry No-No. It's only February and you've maxed out your shenanigans for the year."

Noel stares me down like she can pull off the whole menacing mean girl thing. She can't. The girl is Santa's head elf every holiday season at the mall. With the silly outfit, singing Christmas carols, and entertaining families; she plays the part well.

It also pays well, and she earns a ridiculous amount in cash tips, therefore she doesn't go back to her waitress position at the bar across the street from our apartment until March. Which means her mission to put me in yet another insane situation is full throttle. She's a tiny little demon elf who feeds on chaos and jingle bells.

Handing me a cup of coffee, she waves her hand like I'm being silly. "Oh, Val. You love me too much to truly cut off my crazy." She winks at me before sitting in her fuzzy pink chair. "Besides, you'd be too bored without me around."

My eyebrow lifts at that. While Noel certainly brings most

2

of the mayhem around here, I make my fair share of contributions.

"Okay, not boring. Anyway, there's zero harm in joining a dating app." It's barely eight in the morning and she hasn't stopped pushing this agenda since she woke me up an hour ago, shoving last night's conquest out the door.

"There are several issues with joining a dating app. Starting with unsolicited dick pics. I'll never understand why men assume we want images of their penis. I want to ride it, maybe lick it, but not because it's nice to look at."

We both cringe and shiver at the truth in my words.

"Fair point. Cupid isn't like that though. You connect it to a social media profile to confirm you're an actual human, but you can choose how much information to share. And there are no images. No pictures of man parts or duck lip selfies. It's designed to set you up with someone perfect for you based on a questionnaire you fill out. All you do is pick the time and place you want to meet up."

Yeah, that sounds sketchy as hell. "What happens if there is no physical attraction once I get there?"

Noel smiles as if she's already won. She hasn't, but the only way to get this conversation over with is to make it seem like I've made an informed decision.

"There's a section on the questionnaire for physical and sexual attractions."

I sigh. "I'll think about it, No-No. I've got to get ready for work."

She nods, "Of course. How else would you drool over your bosses today?"

"I do not drool. I'm a fucking lady."

Snorting, she stands up and heads back to her room. Not before turning around and pretending to shoot me with a bow and arrow. There's a sparkle in her eye that tells me she isn't done with Cupid.

I walk into my office with my second cup of coffee this morning and a smile on my face. Not every woman in her mid-twenties can say they love their job and are genuinely happy with their work environment. I work in a male dominated career, but none of my coworkers have ever made me feel less than just because I've got a vagina between my legs.

It's very different from the competitiveness I felt through school. The guys either wanted to fuck me or fuck me over, sometimes both. Even when I said it didn't bother me, there were many nights at the bar with Noel downing shots and bitching about it all.

Ground Up hired me last fall. Most architectural firms are still a bit archaic. I know because I went to over a dozen interviews where I was the only female present. They hire men because construction crews respond better to them. They associate authority with masculinity, meaning jobs run smoother because the contractors don't argue when the orders are coming from someone with a dick.

It's bullshit and change is happening too slowly. Seeing a woman on a job site is still too rare because if they put one in charge, she'd just be called a bitch for doing the exact same role as her counterparts. Probably doing it better, too.

I was lucky to land a spot here, because as much as the company is known for their unique principals, they haven't caught up on workplace diversity. That's something I hope to change in my time here. It may take years of working my way to the top, but I'll make it happen.

The firm works with recycled materials as much as possible, establishes real relationships with our clients, and caters to a teamwork mentality. Meaning douchebags who skate through the hiring process are typically filtered out during the probationary period. Once a month we have an outing for each department for team-building and biweekly meetings with a mentor team.

Scanning my badge through security, I make my way to the elevator bank. I can see one of my coworkers, Chad, waiting in one of the elevators and intentionally slow my steps. Luckily, another one is available, so I hop in.

Unluckily, Chad is waiting when I make it to my floor. I begin walking to my desk, but he follows along.

"Good morning, Val. Looking as beautiful as ever today. Say, I'd hate for you to be lonely this weekend. Come to Chad. Or for Chad. Whatever."

Chad has somehow continued to fly under the radar. He's pretty harmless, but me and the three other women who work for the company try to avoid him for obvious reasons.

I stop and face him. I smile and he thinks his line landed. No way, buddy.

"Oh, Chad. If I wanted to have a mediocre Valentine's weekend by having to ride a tiny dick then hiding in the bathroom after to take care of myself, I'd absolutely take you up on that offer."

A deep chuckle comes from behind me and my face turns red. I probably should have looked around before running my mouth, but it's too late now. Besides, Chad either has a stupid sense of confidence or thinks insults are foreplay because he's still looking at me like he has a chance.

Doesn't make it any better that my boss most likely only heard my response and missed Chad hitting on me. Romeo is one of the owners of Ground Up, the architectural firm I work at. He and his two best friends started the company in college.

Taking a deep breath, I do the mature thing and resign myself to an apology. "Sorry about that, Romeo. Just joking around with a coworker, but I'll refrain from the details next time."

He smiles. "Let me walk you to your desk, Val."

Fuck. I'm barely out of the company probation period. I'm doing a mental tally of my savings with every step to try and see how long I'll be able to afford rent if I get fired. I come to the conclusion that I can make it six months without dipping into the emergency fund if I give up the weekly order of Chinese delivery and one cup of coffee a day.

My mental math is interrupted when I feel a hand on my back. I stumble on my heels, but Romeo helps me balance and I don't fall. I look up and see a smirk on his face though he's looking forward and not at me.

Is this a personal escort to my desk to collect my things? And if he's going to fire, can I get a sexy punishment out of it? Maybe a goodbye spanking is in my future.

Probably not. I'm sure he'll be calling human resources and security before I could bend over.

Chapter Two

Romeo

I shouldn't take so much joy in watching Val squirm, but I can't help it. We've been watching her since the first day and there's no question that we all want her. Too bad she's our employee.

The day of her interview, I thought there would be a brawl. As soon as she left, all three of us already had a pro and con list. She's absolutely gorgeous and all of us were enamored right away. The minute the office door closed behind her, we had a very rare argument. Hart didn't want to hire her, Beau and I did.

Ultimately, Hart lost. And not just for someone to eye fuck around here, but because she would be a true asset to our company. Her school portfolio could speak for itself.

Her intelligence and drive shine through her eyes.

Eyes that I want to watch glaze over while I'm on top of her, amongst other things I'm not allowed to be thinking about.

Leave it to Hart to give us all a reminder that we can't exactly fuck an employee, especially one like Val. She's proved herself through the mandatory probation period. Her mentors and department heads have raved about her. They have been requesting her for every project opening we've had in the last month.

That's something we've been discussing in the top chain too. We are still a smaller firm with around two hundred employees throughout the entire company. Hart, Beau, and I oversee everything. Especially project management.

Which is why I'm really down here. Not to give her shit for putting Chad in his place. I'll have to tell the guys about it though, we need to keep an eye on him.

Val and I reach her desk and she takes a seat, while I stand and lean against the file cabinet that makes up part of her cubicle.

"Quite the comment you made to Chad back there, Val." I couldn't help but laugh at her joke, but now I'm a little annoyed that she might know his dick size from personal reference.

There's a blush working its way up her skin, covering her neck and cheeks. "I'm sorry about that, sir. It was meant to be a joke."

"Sir" isn't really my thing. Hart, though, he'd love to hear it.

"I'm sure he earned it. Really, don't worry about it." I wink at her to lighten the mood, but it doesn't work. She's still tense.

"Was there something else you needed, sir?" I love her voice. And her face. And her beautiful fucking brain.

Yes, Val. There are many things I need.

I'd like to hear you call my best friend sir in the board-room just to see if his eyes light up or if he has to adjust himself under the table. I need to convince you to go out with me. I need to convince myself that you wouldn't look perfect on your knees right here, right now. I wonder if she'd let me climb under the desk and hide between her legs for the next hour. Or two. I could clear my calendar.

Shaking my head to clear out that beautiful picture, I focus on what I came down here for.

"Nothing too important. We have a big project coming up. It's a complete redesign and restructure with predominantly green materials and the potential for a national contract."

We can stand against the larger firms, but a contract like that could take us outside of the city and state into the entire country. We've been talking it over and are all in agreement that Val would be a perfect addition to the team.

There's a spark in her eyes that tells me we picked the right person. "We'd like you to join the team."

I could have waited until she had finished sipping her coffee to drop that on her. Instead, she chokes on it and tries to avoid spitting up on herself. A rational man would have grabbed the handkerchief from his suit pocket to hand over.

I am not a rational man.

That's why my hand is currently under her chin trying to catch anything that may come up like a beggar waiting for scraps.

I am unworthy of my own name at this moment. There was never a less swoony moment than this. Kill me now and on my tombstone label me a complete fucking weirdo.

"Umm, thanks?" Val sounds as mortified as I feel.

I stand and dust off the lapels of my suit like I've just completed a hard day's work and have nothing to be embarrassed about. Fake it until you make it.

"You bet. Always happy to be a helping hand." If there was a quicksand pit beneath my feet, I'd let it eat me whole. Let a mythological giant snake pop out and devour me. Maybe a sniper is waiting to take me out. "Anyways, what do you think?"

Val stares at me for another moment before snapping out of it, a giant smile lighting up her face. "I think that would be awesome. Am I just observing?"

What can I do to get this girl to smile like that for me again? I'd sell my damn soul for it. It's not the polite forced smile she gave in her interview or when I've seen her in meetings. This smile could move mountains. Baby Jesus would weep graciously.

Who the fuck am I right now? I'm a fucking badass. Alpha-male. A real specimen of manliness. Why am I dreaming of my employee's damn smile and how it would bring a tiny human prophet to tears?

"How about I reserve some time on your email calendar for you to come upstairs and we can talk about expectations, then?" Look at me, being professional as fuck even though I can't take my eyes off her mouth.

Realizing I'm staring intently, I nod as if she gave me confirmation and make my way back to my office.

Chapter Three

Hart

The sound of Beau wheezing from laughing at Romeo's antics should be annoying me, but instead I find myself chuckling at our friend too.

"Were you trying to catch her drool? Or looking for a handout?" Beau isn't going to let this go for years. If it weren't for him and Romeo, I doubt I'd even know what life outside of this office is. They remind me to leave the building and step away from work. We tell our employees that balance is healthy which means we have to set the example that often has them nagging me.

I like to pretend it's annoying, but I'm grateful. I love this company and my job, but I don't want it to own me. We're all in our early thirties and own our own firm. We make a fucking difference in this industry and eventually, the world will see it too.

Romeo groans while tilting his head toward the ceiling. "Like you fuckers have any room to talk. Why were you both watching her desk to begin with?"

"Because Hart is a stalker." The chuckling stops and I

remember that I hate them both as much as I love them. All those nice things I was just thinking cease to exist.

Beau might have walked in while I was checking to see that Val made it in on time. Sometimes I do that. It's the best part of having access to all the security cameras throughout the building. They can't blame me for being resourceful.

"As a leader in this company, I take the safety of my employees seriously." That's what I say, but the truth is the only person I check in on is Val. I'd never admit it to them though.

The looks they are giving me prove they call bullshit.

I'm aware we all feel drawn to her. It's the same calling we saw in each other in college. Respect, desire for knowledge, and determination.

Instead of setting ourselves against each other, we learned quickly that allies were more important. It helped that the first project we were assigned together was a challenge from our professor to build a project from the ground up that used recycled materials. It was clear we all shared the passion of sustainability as well as the competitive drive to blow the other groups out of the water.

We solidified our group because of that project and haven't stopped working to build things together since. Ground Up included.

"What is the plan for this weekend?" Changing the subject works in my favor. I need something to take my mind off the fact that Romeo arranged a meeting with Val later this afternoon without clearing it with me first.

Not because I needed to rearrange my schedule, which I did, but because I don't have time to mentally prepare to be in the same room with her.

Beau is the first to break, finally forgetting their stalker banter from before. "It's Valentine's Day. It's the one weekend a month I'd rather drown in scotch than go out and see the love vomit all over town."

"I disagree. Where there is love vomit, there are sad girls who need to be reminded they are beautiful." Leave it to Romeo to be romantic. Especially when we all know not one of us has stopped thinking about the girl who works a few floors below us since the day she walked into this building for her interview.

Most weekends we hang out at our townhouse. Working and living together should seem like too much, but we rarely bicker over anything and never anything important.

Women, different ideas at the workplace, family matters; we work everything out and keep each other honest.

Except for when it comes to Val. I might have been the one to declare her off limits because of the dynamic here in the office, not to mention being in a position of power over her, but I won't battle it out with my best friends over a girl we shouldn't be dating in the first place.

Sighing, I check the calendar. Honestly, until it was mentioned, I didn't realize the date. Not that any of us have had a recent relationship worth remembering the holiday for anyways. "I've got nothing on my personal agenda for the weekend or holiday. I do, however, have a call with a client in a few minutes."

A call I rescheduled so we can meet with the subject we are all thinking about. A call I have no interest in taking when I could be in a room with her instead.

"He's kicking us out and leaving us on our own, Beau." Romeo stands and puts his arm out for Beau, pulling him to his feet too.

"At least we still have each other, Romeo. I'm no Juliet, but I bet I'd look pleasant in a gown. Do you want to be my Valentine?" He spins around and curtsies as they make their way to the door.

I roll my eyes as they shuffle out of my office being loud and absurd. "Get some damn work done, will you?"

Their laughs travel down the hallway with them. Assholes.

Chapter Four

Val

The fifteen-minute warning goes off on my computer and I prepare myself for a meeting about this new project. I'm not sure who else is joining the team, but I have no doubt that the bosses will be monitoring every step closely.

I take a few minutes to use the bathroom and freshen up my appearance before grabbing my laptop, a notepad, and two pens. I always have two pens for notes because there's a chance that the first one will stop working. While I could take notes on my laptop, it's hard for me to focus while staring at the screen. Besides, there is a heavy sense of achievement every time I can physically check something off a list.

When I've made it upstairs, my nerves ramp up. Maybe because when I walk into the room, every single wet dream I've ever had about workplace sexual escapades couldn't come close to the sight in front of me.

Romeo. Hart. Beau.

Each of them stands to greet me with panty dropping smiles.

Speaking of panties, I'll need new ones.

How does one end up with three bosses who look like they should be on the covers of romance novels? No idea.

Bodies? Rideable.

Faces? Sittable.

Dicks? I haven't seen them, but I'm betting they are fuckable. Or lickable.

What more could you ask for?

"Thank you for making time to meet with us, Val. I've set a document on the table that we will need you to review and sign." Hart's voice is always authoritative. It's only been directed at me a couple of times before, during the interview process and once when he was giving a speech about the workplace at my new hire orientation.

I take a seat and begin reading the page on the desk. It's a non-disclosure agreement. I look up at Hart and raise a brow.

I get a smirk out of him, but it quickly slips back to business. "It's necessary for the project we are on. We cannot even tell you the name of the company without it, per the client's wishes."

I love his voice. It's commanding, sure, but there's something soft hidden underneath. It's as if he could boss me around then play with my hair while I fall asleep on his shoulder.

Scanning the document, I pretend to understand all the legal jargon and sign my name at the bottom.

Romeo scoops it up quickly and places it in a file. "Perfect. Glad to have you on our team, Val." He's much smoother now than he was earlier this morning, his signature smirk still in place.

Clearing my throat, I ask, "The client?"

"Winter Wonderland Corporations." Hart answers, tone as direct as ever.

They own the Christmas Town set up that Noel works for. Interesting.

Beau takes over, opening a laptop and setting it in front of me. His specialty is urban design and he's damn good at it. The firm has had articles in several magazines because of his designs.

"They want to do a complete remodel across the country, starting here in the city. We have the next eight months to design, demo, and rebuild. Winter Wonderland is testing us with one location. If we succeed, we get the national contract with potential for global designs in the future."

I nod along as he shows me the several concept ideas they have so far.

"It's imperative that we take this on and exceed all expectations. They want to be the nation's largest holiday celebration station and they think going green with the materials will give them an unbeatable edge." Romeo adds.

Sustainability and environmentally friendly don't always go hand in hand. Over the years, he's pushed the boundaries and called out for companies to try and do the same. Last year, the National Architectural Accrediting Board gave him an award and asked him to give a keynote speech on how to start taking the approach of going green across the industry.

Hart has stayed silent while the other two fill me in. He watches me closely. He's the financial guy. We take a lot of risks to do what we do, the biggest being the money. Hart runs the company and the cash to keep us turning a good profit.

I don't have a clear idea of each role or details of what their day-to-day duties are, but each one of them has made their own waves in this business.

"Can I ask why I'm here? Is it for me to observe? Because I'd be lucky to just do that." I mean it too. A project of this magnitude, most new architects would be grateful to set foot on the job site.

"We want you to lead the interiors team." Hart says it as if it's completely reasonable.

"That makes no sense." Shouldn't have said that.

Hart raises a brow, but Romeo and Beau both chuckle.

"Not that you aren't very smart men capable of making reasonable decisions." That's better. "What I mean is there are tenured team members who would undoubtedly have more experience for a project of this size and importance."

"You can handle it, Val." Romeo's smile is reassuring, but his words have me wondering what else he could let me handle. I bet he'd say those same words right before thrusting into me.

They all have big dick energy for damn sure.

I have to physically shake these thoughts from my head so I can focus.

"We'll be here to help every step of the way. We don't expect you to be perfect, I promise. There will be challenges, long days and even nights, but we trust you can do it." Oh, I could totally do them for long nights. Nope, focus. "Besides, you'll have an entire team behind you."

Beau's words are confident and kind and I'm nodding along in agreement before I can stop myself. His reassurance means a lot to me. If he tells me I could do something, I could absolutely conquer it. And if I couldn't, he'd be right beside me to help.

Then again, when he says team, I hear train. And now I'm thinking about my bosses running a train on me. Is that on everyone's fantasy list or just mine? Only with them though. It's the group dynamic the three of them have going on. Their teamwork makes my wet dreams work.

Once I'm sure thoughts of being railed by the people signing my paychecks are not reflected on my face, I look at

Hart. I'm not expecting words of comfort from him, and I don't get any.

"We'll set up another meeting next week. There are several trusted individuals within your department and we can collaborate to create the best team for you and the project."

Standing up, I offer each of them a polite handshake. "Thank you. I'm nervous, but more than anything, I am very excited to take this on."

Could I take on all of you, too?

I practically run to my desk before I can start stripping off my clothes to lay on the table and demanding they ravish me. I'm a bad bitch and I've got work to do.

Chapter Five

Beau

My friends are going to think it's a stupid idea, but I want to do something for Valentine's Day. I know we are all fighting our attraction to Val and they need to get over it.

Or I need to push them into an uncomfortable situation so they will realize that we are all grown adults and can be attracted to a woman in the workplace who can make her own decision on whether she'd like to give any of us a chance.

I'm not an idiot. Val is attracted to all of us. When she walked into our meeting earlier, she had the same lust in her eyes that we all did.

I've known Romeo and Hart for years. Not one of us would begrudge the other for finding someone that makes them happy. If that someone is Val, awesome. If not, at least they tried.

If it worked out for someone? It'd be the best thing that happened since starting Ground Up. No matter who she picked, they'd make beautiful genius architect babies. If she wanted to.

Maybe it would be me.

I need to pause those thoughts. I've got a mission and it's important they agree.

Walking out of my bedroom, I see them both in the kitchen trying to decide what to order in. Occasionally we take turns cooking, but not often.

"I've made our plans for Valentine's Day. If you'll check your email, there's a link to fill out a questionnaire." I announce and pick up the menu for our usual Chinese restaurant.

"Why the hell would we do that?" Romeo asks while pulling out his phone to order our usual from the restaurant's website.

Clasping my hands in front of me, I stare them both down. "Here's the deal. I'm making an executive decision. The Cupid dating app is hosting a singles event."

Hart is shaking his head, but I continue. "It's happening. Even if we go and get hammered at the bar because our dates don't work out, we still get out of the house for the first time in months."

I'm making a good point and they know it. We've been so busy with work and the new clientele that we've been spending even the weekends in the office. It's not healthy.

"Fuck it, I'm in." Romeo pats me on the shoulder. "I'm going to shower, but the food should be here in about twenty minutes."

One down.

"No."

Hart to be a buzzkill isn't unexpected. "Sorry, two against one. The friendship book says you have to take one for the team."

I snicker as I watch him take his phone from his pocket and open up his email. Hart knows he could tell me to fuck off and I wouldn't push anymore. He also knows that we're all torn up over the same girl and need to find a healthy way to get over it.

"Damn it. If I get set up with some weirdo with a foot fetish, you have to pick up my dry cleaning for the next month." He's already filling out the questionnaire, typing aggressively against his screen.

Holding out my fist for a bump, he meets me. "Deal."

Chapter Six

Val

"**D**on't get mad." Noel is standing in front of our door waiting for me when I get home from work. The innocent look on her face doesn't deter me one bit. "What did you do?"

"If you really think about it, the only person you should be upset with is yourself. You chose me as your best friend in elementary school. You've trusted me with your personal information. You let me know all your kinks and quirks. Most importantly, you've never changed your password."

Her hands are on her hips and her tone is serious, even though she's out of breath from her speech.

"Yes, well clearly my taste in friends is flawed since you're the only one I have. I'll own up to trusting you with sensitive information. Now, what the hell have you done?"

She's grinning so big I can see exactly why kids think she's really an elf from the North Pole. "I scored you a date for Valentine's Day."

"No. I'm not going on a blind date. Cancel it." It's a disaster waiting to happen. I'd much rather stay home in pajamas, eating cheesecake that I have delivered to my door, and wearing my favorite fuzzy socks.

Noel is pouting, but I'm not buying it. "I mean it, No-No. I'm not interested." She's pushier than usual, but I'm standing my ground this time around.

"Let me explain." She runs to the kitchen and pours me a glass of wine. The bottle was twenty bucks, that's fancy for us. Even though we both make decent money, we don't always splurge on the little things.

"Wine first. No more words until the Moscato is consumed, please." I won't survive her antics otherwise.

She hands me a glass where I'm sitting cross legged on the couch and sits across from me in her chair. "Don't interrupt me, okay? I'm really excited and I want you to be too."

I'm too busy gulping down the adult grape juice to interrupt her. It's cold and sweet and just what I need.

"I signed you up for Cupid."

To be fair, I'm not sure that spraying the wine in my mouth at her was something I could have prevented. You can't drop a bomb like that casually and not expect a reaction. It's her fault.

"You did what?" I'm shouting at her. Loudly. Because what the hell is wrong with her?

"That's fucking gross, Valley girl. And I haven't finished explaining." Wiping her face with her shirt, she straightens up in her chair. "Not the app, not really. I signed us both up for their Valentine's single event. I filled out your questionnaire, because of course I know all the answers anyway."

I shrug. She isn't wrong, we've had many talks about our attractions and desires. Just like we both dreamed we would marry Justin Timberlake and be sister wives.

"They text you the address the day of. They take their compatibility technology and use the questionnaire to match

CUPID IS A C*NT

you for the night. You know who your match is because they hand you a symbol and you have to seek them out."

"What if my match is a woman?" I'm not saying that I'm going, but I need to know regardless.

Noel rolls her eyes. "First, don't knock it until you try it. Second, under your preferences, I listed that you prefer male companions."

"I have tried it; you were there a time or two. And thank you, but it's a no." Back in college, I did experiment with my sexuality more than once. Noel and I took our youth and freedom seriously. Something I grew out of, and she didn't. I'm very open minded, but I do prefer men.

"Val, please. You haven't made an effort to get laid in months, you've been focused on the new job. It's time to dust the cobwebs off the clit and get lit."

Shaking my head, I vehemently insist it's a no.

THE GOLDEN ARROW.

I'm staring up at the club whose brick walls are painted with a stark black most likely named cliche.

I really wanted to wear my usual little black dress, but Noel convinced me to put on a pink dress made of slinky material and sequins. After convincing me to do this in the first place. It makes me look like a disco ball, but that didn't stop me from shimmying around in front of my mirror to see the pretty colors in full effect before hopping into an Uber to get here.

Conveniently, she had a stomach bug tonight and couldn't make it.

DREA DENAE

I am a bad bitch. I can do shit on my own. I can also get drunk and order myself an Uber. I've got this.

That's the pep talk I give myself as I walk into the club. My eyes take a minute to adjust to the dark. There's a woman and a man standing behind a booth, both wearing masks.

"Good evening, can we have a form of identification please?"

I hand over my license, assuming they're checking my age. Instead, they scan it.

"Oh hello. We've been waiting for you." The woman says it politely, but it's still creepy. "My name is Desire. This is Pleasure." She points to the man beside her.

"Why?" I'm on guard, but I'm going to shake off the weird vibes and hope this is how they are greeting all of tonight's guests. I have no idea what I'm about to walk into and it's making me more anxious with every passing moment.

"I have your symbol here. I'm very excited for you." This time the man speaks.

I pin the rose to my dress and walk over to the curtain. Looking back at the odd couple, they are watching me and nodding in awe. "Please, find us if we can service you in any manner."

So, I go forward, if only to escape them.

When I take in the scene ahead of me, I wish I ran. Fuck Noel. This is definitely the last time I do anything she suggests.

There's a stage with a St. Andrew's cross. In the corner I see a leather sectional big enough to host an orgy. A very wavy chaise lounge as well as other odd furniture is all over the place.

There are plenty of fully dressed people making casual conversation, some with matching symbols and others who keep eyeing the curtain waiting for their own.

I make my way to the bar, where I see three men waiting. The bartender comes over and I order a glass of red wine while I try to look for their symbols. I'm unable to see and all three are clearly arguing and standing tensely, huddled together. When it's clear that I won't be getting an eye of their symbols, I decide to find a booth in the corner.

I can still see everyone and people watch to my heart's desire. Men and women with other men and women all getting to know each other as if we aren't currently at the sexfest headquarters.

Due to my nerves, I drink my first glass faster than I wanted and I find myself walking back to the bar for another. Two is tonight's limit, I can't risk getting too tipsy or I might be climbing that fancy cross like it's a stripper pole.

This time as I approach the bar, I see the three men from earlier still there. They no longer seem to be engrossed in their conversation and are instead now looking for their matches. Except these men aren't strangers. One at a time, I make eye contact with my bosses.

Fuck.

Beau. Hart. Romeo.

It couldn't be at a normal bar or even a decent restaurant. Nope, it had to be a sex club on Valentine's Day.

And if that wasn't enough, all three are wearing a rose symbol identical to mine.

Chapter Seven

Hart

W hen we arrived at the club and each of us received the same symbol, I demanded to speak with someone in charge. Was this sham of a dating company setting me up with my best friends?

It wouldn't be completely off base. As friends, we're obviously compatible, but to my knowledge we all prefer women. When one of the hosts explained there was no mistake, I wanted to leave. Considering they've set us all up in place meant for sexual debauchery, I assumed they were hoping we'd participate as a throuple.

Then she explained our match wasn't here yet. That all three of us were equally matched to the same person.

Now we are all sitting here waiting for whoever this person is to appear. Then we watch a gorgeous figure decked out in pink sequins rush through the curtain.

Well, fuck.

"Dibs, you fuckers can go home. If our date shows up, she still gets the two of you and I'll wish you all a throuple of happiness." Beau starts walking her way, but Romeo and I grab him by the collar and pull him back to us.

"No. Absolutely not. She's still our employee, even outside the office." I can't lose this battle. The whole point of coming out to this miserable event was to maybe meet someone else. Maybe being the strong word, because regardless of who walked through that curtain, we all would have ended up back at our place sans blind dates.

"I'm done. I played by the rules, but fate has intervened. The arrow to my heart is linked to hers." Even for Romeo, that sounds ridiculous.

Only then do I see the symbol she's wearing.

"Huddle." They both look back at me, unamused. "Fucking huddle up. We need a game plan."

I never could have imagined that Val was in the same system we had signed up for. Or that one of us would match with her, let alone all three.

Wrapping my arm around their shoulders, I pull them towards me. We look absurd, but she shouldn't be able to identify us yet.

We can all feel her presence as she approaches the bar and orders a drink.

"We can't." It's starting to sound unconvincing, even to me.

Beau smacks me upside the head and I grunt. "It's time to let go of that mentality and realize we've been given a chance."

I'm being swayed towards something I'm tired of fighting.

"You mean I've been given a chance. I think you should both leave." Romeo earns himself a smack this time.

This has been my biggest worry. As much as I do believe in the imbalance of power should Val enter into a relationship with us, I'm worried about my friends more.

Beau speaks next. "I need to know something. Is this about dating her or fucking her. We all answer on the count of three. One, two, three."

"Both." If Romeo and Beau are surprised my answer matches theirs, they don't show it.

Damn it. I'm done with this. "Fine. We need a plan. What the hell do we do?"

We all tense up in our huddle. Val has her drink in hand and is looking around. Finally, she walks to the other side of the room and sits down.

"Let's let her pick." Beau, the reasonable one tonight, apparently.

"Obviously it has to be her choice, but what do we do? Approach her as a group and flex? Show off our dicks? You know I'd win." This time Romeo almost breaks our huddle as he gets smacked on both sides of his head.

"Shut the hell up. No contest." I'm the boss. I think of the plans and then I ensure they are executed flawlessly. "Here's what we are going to pitch, then let her decide."

I lay it all out and ask if there are any questions. "So we are all in agreement?"

They nod in confirmation.

"Perfect timing. She's headed our way." Beau had the best vantage point to keep an eye on her booth.

"Here we go, boys."

Breaking our huddle, we stand side by side. The shock on her face is clear and I see her eyes look to the curtain marking the entrance and exit of the club.

Now that we're here though, she's not getting away so easily.

"Val." I step forward and Romeo and Beau do as well. "You're our match."

Saying that feels right, no matter how unorthodox the rest of this experience has been.

"Holy fucking shit." She's clearly overwhelmed, reasonably so. Not only are we in this ridiculous club under the pretense of a blind set up, but we also aren't strangers. We are her employers.

"Cupid is a cunt."

"Excuse me?" I'm surprised by her outburst.

Val tosses her hands up. "I mean it. First, they collect all this personal information from me. I mean technically, Noel filled it out and as much as I hate to say it out loud, I'm sure she did so with complete accuracy."

I look to my friends who are just as confused. Romeo's brow wrinkles. "Who is Noel?"

"My best friend and roommate. She convinced me this was a great idea because we could do it together. What I would do in order to trade places with her right now. Fucking stomach bug. So then she tells me to put on this dress." Her hands move up and down in front of her showing off her very sparkly dress.

Beau chuckles at her. "I'm going to have to give her a point. It's a great dress."

She doesn't like that. Val growls. Actually growls. No points for anyone, except maybe her. It sounds like a tiny kitten, but we all act intimidated.

"Total twat. Got it." Beau earns himself a small smirk from her.

Val isn't done though. "Then I'm here in what is undoubtedly a sex dungeon kink performance arena. Not that I'm judging. I'm not. Really. Kink shaming is absolute bullshit and not okay. It's just you'd think they'd warn you. Were they expecting people to just show up and start fucking each other? I mean I'm sure we've all fucked strangers before and yes, in the right moment, public sex is hot as sin."

"Wait, what?"

"How public?"

"What is kink shaming?"

Clearly, Romeo and Beau are just as confused as I am.

"Then there's the creepy couple at the front who I'm pretty sure will be leading a naked conga line at some point tonight." Finally, something we understand. The odd couple at the front.

"And I show up to not one blind date, but three. All of whom are my fucking bosses. Cupid is an absolute dirty fucking cunt."

Val is really upset and all I want to do is calm her down, but I don't want to overwhelm her any more than she already is.

"Let's just take a seat and talk. I know this is a lot, and we are just as shocked at the situation as you are, believe me. We had a serious discussion with the organizer when we arrived. We're here, though."

The fact that we've all kept our cool, to a certain degree, is mind-blowing. This place is insane. I'm pretty sure a waitress is walking around with a tray full of lube and another with condoms.

I motion to my friends. "You guys go find a table and I'll grab us drinks. Val, what would you like?"

Her chest rises and falls. For a minute, I think she might continue with her feelings about the mess we're in, but I'm glad she chooses not to. "Red wine."

"Perfect. I'll meet you over there." I decide to be forward and kiss her cheek. Her eyes go wide, but I'm already moving toward the bar.

Watching as the other two lead her back to her booth, I go over the plan in my head. There's no way of knowing that she will go for it, but hopefully it will work.

I order our drinks and point out our table to the bartender. I won't be able to carry all the glasses myself, so a waitress is getting them organized on a tray to bring them over.

I'm over to the booth and sliding in beside Beau only a

few seconds before our drinks are delivered. Since I closed out our tab at the bar, assuming Val was ready to run from this place, I take out a bill to tip the waitress.

Once we have privacy, I get right to the point. "Give us the weekend."

"Umm, what?" Val takes a drink from her glass.

"I think the best thing to do here is be honest." I glance at my friends. Beau is already in agreement judging by the smile on his face and Romeo begrudgingly gives me a nod.

I grab one of her hands that's currently fidgeting with her wine glass. "The three of us have been interested in you since you walked into Ground Up months ago. We want you. Until now, we've kept our distance because it seemed like the right thing to do. I think I speak for all of us that knowing an anonymous computer application grouping us together as compatible is a turn of events we're grateful for."

"He's right. As usual. I don't know how it happened, but I'm not displeased in the slightest. Now that we're here, together, I couldn't have imagined a better outcome." Romeo sounds formal, but I know how much he means it.

Beau doesn't wait to throw out his own agreement. "I'd consider myself the luckiest son of bitch in this place. Including that guy over there."

"Wait a minute. Is he laughing? While being restrained in those medieval looking stocks?" Val asks.

"Yes, but the point is he looks very happy. I am happier because I'm with you." Beau's statement has her melting in her seat.

I'd like to speed this along before any other scenes begin. "Stay with us for the weekend. We can spend some more time together, get to know each other, whatever you want."

Now that things are really getting going in the club, Val starts to get distracted. "I fucking knew there would be orgies."

Romeo coughs. "Yes, well, I'd imagine more…group activities are likely."

There's both fear and curiosity in Val's eyes now. I reach my hand over the booth and cup her face to draw her attention back to me.

"When the weekend is over, you'll know who you want to explore things with. Whoever it is, they will be so damn happy, Val. And whoever it isn't, they'll still be happy. No hard feelings." As I say the words, I know they are true, except maybe the hard feelings.

Losing out on a chance to really date Val…it's something I don't want to think about right now.

"He's right. Please don't leave here tonight and make us all go back to seeing you in the office as just a woman we work with," Beau adds.

Romeo grabs her other hand. "You're much more than that. Give us a chance to get to know you for real and we will all do the same. If you leave now all we will have left is the what ifs."

Chapter Eight

Val

Rushing into the bathroom, I dial Noel. I'm a chicken shit and need to call my best friend to help me make this very adult decision.

"Ugh, I'm trying to stop dry heaving, call back later." The fact that she really was sick today is the only reason I'm not calling up a modern-day witch to cast a spell on her for leaving me on my own tonight.

"It's them!" I whisper shout into the phone.

"Who?" She whispers back as if someone besides me could hear her through the phone.

"My bosses. I matched with my bosses. All three of them."

I'm still not sure how this happened. I've been crushing on them for months, letting dirty thoughts eat away at my intelligence. Not that anyone besides Noel knows that. The chances of our compatibility doesn't surprise me, but the fact that they are here and even signed up to begin with does.

Noel gasps. "It's a Valentine's miracle, you lucky bitch."

"It's a disaster." I will not let her turn this into some cute situation. "They want me to spend the weekend with them and then pick one of them. They're insane."

"That makes perfect sense." There's not an ounce of sarcasm in her raspy tone.

My hand smacks my forehead as I groan into the phone. "What the hell do you mean?"

"I can't imagine a better opportunity to have hot sex and test your compatibility. Do it."

Well, when you put it like that....

"Absolutely not. I can't spend an entire weekend with my bosses, doing heaven knows what." Them. I'd be doing them. There's zero doubt in my mind that I would not even try to control myself if they showed me a patch of skin. I bet even their wrists are sexy. I sigh. "What is wrong with you?"

And then what? I'd go back to the office Monday and expect to be taken seriously? Would we pretend that nothing ever happened?

Not to mention that I could end the weekend deciding to actually date one of them. If they still wanted me anyways.

"Val, there's nothing wrong with an adventure. Even if it's scary. Hell, the best adventures always are. If you're not almost peeing your pants with worry, it's probably not worth it."

Noel's logic is incredibly flawed, so why am I considering it?

"So, you all live together?"

Yes, I went home with them. After bickering with Noel for ten minutes, I left the bathroom and decided to just go for it.

If I end up jobless because of this weekend, Noel has

agreed to support me financially. Even if that means she has to sell pictures of her feet on the internet.

They have a townhouse in a great part of town. It's an open floor plan and I can tell they've made it their own. At the entry way I spotted the same type of thermostat we have at the office. It's a smart design built to conserve energy when there is less population in the building during off hours.

The LED lighting and appliances are also energy efficient. Because interiors is my specialty, it's easy to spot that while there are plenty of remodeled areas of the home, they've also tried to keep as much of the original build as possible. I admire that they practice in their home what they preach professionally.

I live with my best friend so it shouldn't be so surprising that three grown men also share a home, but even with the business being small, they must make a good enough profit to own their own places.

"It's easier that way. Cost effective, too." Hart tells me this as he helps me out of my coat before leading me through the rest of the place. I nod in understanding.

With my salary, I could probably afford my own place, but it makes much more sense to live with Noel. Besides, I think I'd be lonely if that little demon elf weren't constantly getting me wrapped up in her shenanigans.

Romeo places his hand on my lower back. "Would you like to see the rest of the place?"

"Maybe she'd like something to drink? Or eat? We could order something." Beau steps in front of me. He has a huge smile on his face and is bouncing in place just a bit, like a happy puppy.

I can't help but smile back. "I could use a drink. Just another glass of red, if you have it."

He nods before working his way through the kitchen.

"You guys want your usual?" He looks to Hart and Romeo who both give him a nod.

While Beau sets about getting our drinks, I let Romeo lead me into their living area. The space is open with a plush couch and coffee table in the center. Their television is mounted on the wall and encased in a frame.

The part I love most is that even though the space is big, it still feels comfy. A sense of home washes over me as I take a seat. Beau is quick with my wine, and I take a large drink before looking down at the glass.

Now that we're all just sitting here, I feel a tad bit awkward.

"Can I ask what you all had in mind for this weekend? I'm guessing it's not a creepy attempt to kidnap me and hold me hostage, but you should know I've told my friend Noel exactly who I am with and sent her my location."

And now it's even more awkward. At least, until all three of them laugh.

Romeo scoots closer to me and places his hand on my knee. "I'm glad you thought about your safety, love."

That endearment is sweet to my ears but seems to feel very slippery as it works its way down to my panties.

There is one thing I'm curious about. I really do believe that matching with them was a strange coincidence, and while I don't think they have nefarious motives for asking me here, I want to make sure.

"Quick question. Did you guys lure me here to fuck me as some sort of reward for giving me a lead role on the new project?"

It's silent for a solid second. Clearly, I've caught them off guard because they're all staring at me until the sound of shattering glass breaks them out of it.

Beau doesn't seem to mind that his drink is now all over

the floor instead of still in his hand. Each man looks horrified at my question, but I had to make sure.

Romeo's hand on my knee tightens, almost painfully, but not intentionally.

"What?" Hart's voice is harsh. "Do you really think that?"

I don't, but I can see how offended they are. Shaking my head, I look down at my glass. "No."

"If you want to leave, Val, you can. We want you to stay, but not if there's any doubt in your mind of why you're here." Romeo loosens his grip on my knee.

I realize the question was insulting, but if I hadn't asked, then I'd be letting the toxic thought sit in the back of my mind every second I'm here.

Beau is still frozen in place, but Hart stands up and approaches me. Crouching down, he eyes Romeo's hand on my leg. There's not a visible reaction and his friend doesn't move away.

Hart's hands cup both my cheeks. "I need you to understand that we would never, ever take advantage of any person in that way. It's important to me that you know this. To all of us."

Taking my time, I let my eyes wander over all three, even though my head is still cradled in a pair of hands. Romeo and Hart seem calm enough, but Beau has risen to his feet and his mortification makes me feel a tinge of guilt.

I take a deep breath and slowly exhale before smiling. "I know. I didn't mean to imply that you're a bunch of creepy predator dudes, but I didn't want any doubt in my mind this weekend. So, what exactly is your plan?"

The relief is palpable throughout the room. Hart frees my face from his embrace, but I already miss it. He moves back to his spot on the large couch.

"We don't really have much of a plan. I do think we

should work out the sleeping arrangements. We have a small guest room if that would be more comfortable."

More comfortable than what? Each of them is wearing a cocky smirk and it takes me a moment to work out what the alternative sleeping arrangement is.

Oh….

"Cuddles. I want all the cuddles." Beau's voice is calm and confident, shaking off the last of his earlier nerves. As he does, he remembers the mess on the ground from his dropped drink. "Oh, shit."

He moves to grab the supplies to clean it up which he makes quick work of. The certainty of his request makes me laugh.

Cuddles.

Romeo sits back, his hand leaving my knee but moving up to twirl a lock of my hair. "Don't start with your demands, Beau. We have to find a way to make it equal or we'll have to accept that Val will be spending the night in the guest room instead of our beds."

Yeah, they want me to sleep with them. Sleep like sleep. Not like fuck. Although…is that on the table?

"Keeping it fair is important. Otherwise, we aren't giving Val a real chance to know us." Hart says.

Beau snorts. "You're both talking about Val and her time as if she isn't in the room, assholes."

He makes a great point. One I would have made myself if he hadn't beat me to it. The other two do seem to realize their mistake and give me sheepish looks before apologizing.

"I'm open to other arrangements." I say this calmly, as if I'm not thinking of lying beside them. On top of them. Underneath them. "What are you thinking?"

My head turns to Hart naturally. Not because his opinion matters more than Beau or Romeo's, but because he seems to think logically. And even though this weekend is essentially a test between the three of them to find who I'd consider dating in the future, there's no sense of competition.

I respect that. I'd be less interested in this situation if there was any chance of them fighting over me as if I'm the last weapon in a battle to the death.

Although, if that were a thing, I'd request the Roman battle gear. Like Gerard Butler in *300*.

"We should try to split up our time," Hart states and his friends agree. "When she's with one of us, that person and Val can decide what they would like to do. As long as she's comfortable and safe, which is a given, then I think we can all agree that is fair."

Beau is nodding, but adds, "I don't want it to be weird around here. We don't have to hide out in our rooms. I'll get a grocery order delivered tomorrow. Val, any specific requests or allergies?"

His phone is already out with the notepad open. "No allergies. I don't eat very healthy food, but I don't hate fruits and vegetables either. I'm warning you now, though, caffeine is a necessity."

This gets a laugh from all three of them. "Oh, we know."

That last comment comes from Romeo and when I raise my eyebrow at him, he just shrugs and winks. "Don't worry, our machine here is really good and we can order in if needed."

Thank goodness. I'm not too picky about my coffee, so I'm sure their machine will be fine.

And maybe I should be a little more nervous, but they've done everything they can to make sure I'm comfortable here. I'm spending the weekend with three men I barely know. Three very hot and handsome men who just so happen to sign my paychecks. Monday's Val can worry about it, that's her problem.

I nod. "It's been a long night. So, who is the lucky guy tonight? Wait, I'm only here for two nights, if you don't get tired of me before then. There's three of you. How do we make that work?"

Beau comes over and kisses the top of my head. "We won't be tired of you by then, brownie bite. I tend to stay up late. Insomnia. I'll bow out of the nights and claim a nap with you both afternoons instead."

Is he expecting me to be so worn out from his friends that I'll need to nap? Am I expecting to be worn out by them?

I watch him make his way out of the living area and down the hall, presumably to his room.

Hart clearing his throats brings my attention back. "I'd love to have you to myself tomorrow, Val. If that's alright with Romeo."

The other guy abruptly stops playing with my hair. He looks to his friend and back to me. "Yeah, that sounds good." He stands and helps me to my feet. "Come on, love. I'll show you to my room."

When his hand slips into mine, I intertwine my fingers. Romeo looks down and squeezes gently. Then he smiles.

Chapter Nine

Romeo

With Val's hand in mine, I feel like the luckiest guy in the world. I don't care how cheesy that is. It's a gift that I get to touch her.

Leading her down the hallway, I open my bedroom door. It's clean because I only use it to sleep. We keep work at the office for the most part and I like spending time with the guys around the house. There's a cleaning service that comes by every other week to do the higher maintenance house-work, but none of us have an issue keeping the place tidy.

"I'm not trying to be too forward when I say this, but would you want to get out of that dress?" I walk over to my drawers and pull out a plain shirt and a pair of sweatpants that I know will be too big on her. "You can borrow these. There's a bathroom through that door right there."

We all have our own bathrooms, along with another for guests. That might seem excessive, but it ensures we all have the same privacy and space. It was part of the renovations we did after we bought the place.

Val walks into the bathroom and closes the door behind

her. I go ahead and grab another pair of sweats to change before she's finished.

There's a moment of awkwardness where I consider what side of the bed she would prefer and if she'll be uncomfortable in here. It's over quickly because she walks out a minute later and climbs under the blankets.

She goes to the opposite side of where I normally sleep, and I climb in beside her.

"Do you need anything?" I ask her. Her head shakes in response and I nod. "Let me know if that changes."

We're both sitting with our backs against the headboard. Val looks over and even though the lighting is dim, her nerves are clear on her face. Her hands are fidgeting in her lap.

"Can you tell me something embarrassing, Romeo? I need you to tell me something that evens the playing field for me."

I'm not sure what she means. "What do you need me to do?"

She sighs, but keeps her eyes trained on mine. "Right now, you don't really feel like one of the guys who runs the company I work for, but you aren't exactly a one-night stand either."

The thought of this being a one night only situation makes my chest tighten. Then I remember she's here for at least two. Even if she isn't in bed with me, she's in my house.

"Alright. Something embarrassing will help?"

Val nods. I try to think of the right story, but only one comes to mind. And it surpasses embarrassing. There's a good chance she won't want anything to do with me after this.

"I'm not going to get into the details, because my ego couldn't handle it." I smile at her. Fuck, she's definitely not going to want more than one night with me after this. "Back in college, we had a huge assignment due and we decided to pull an all-nighter. Another group was studying in the same section of the library as us and one of them showed up with a ton of Mexican food."

Her brow slightly raises. I really don't know how she's going to respond to this.

"Long story short, the librarian had locked the bathrooms on that floor when she was getting ready to close up and the closest ones were three floors down. The elevator just happened to be out of order too. Let's just say our study session had to be moved back to our apartment because there was a shituation."

Val seems to be trying to work out the message and I can see the moment the light bulb turns on. She tries to hold in her reactions but fails. Her laughter rings out across the room and soon my own does too.

"Alright, now that I've bared my soul, can I please kiss you?"

She leans over and I take no time slamming my mouth to hers. I want to devour her. Our hands move into each other's hair, over chests. I'm not sure how much time passes, but it's the best kiss of my life.

We get lost in the moment. I pull her with me as I reach over and turn off my lamp and in the dark, we keep memorizing the feel of one another. When it's over, minutes or hours later, I position her back to my front.

I fall asleep being the big spoon for a girl I've been dreaming about for months.

When the sunrise comes through my room, I suddenly

feel anxious. Soon, Val is going to be on Beau's time. He loves his naps, so I'm not surprised at all he claimed afternoons with her.

I don't want to make a big deal out of it either. I just spent all night with her in my arms. The feel of her body pulled into mine reminds me she's still mine until we leave this room.

I can at least give her something to remember later.

Her lips against mine last night made me feel like a teenager, just making out for the fun of it. We never rounded any real bases, instead, I took the time to listen to the little sounds she made every time I moved my lips from her mouth to her jaw or neck. I loved it, but I want more.

Nuzzling against her neck, I give her a kiss on the corner of her collarbone. "Good morning, love."

Val hasn't moved, so I'm guessing she's still asleep. I kiss my way up to her ear before nibbling lightly. Finally, she stirs.

"Coffee or orgasms. That is the only way to wake me up." Her voice is raspy with sleep and I'm not sure if she knows exactly what she's said.

"Permission for option two, please." My mouth continues the journey on her neck, this time downwards and over her shoulder. I'm not about to go any further without her acknowledgement.

She wiggles her ass against me. "Granted."

I can't stop the groan that leaves me, I feel possessed. My hand moves from its spot between her tits and over to cup one firmly. I let my fingers tweak gently at her nipple before pulling harder.

Val pushes herself back against me, looking for more.

"You want something from me, babe? Tell me." My voice is just a whisper in her ear, but I can feel the effect it has on her. The way she slightly shivers in place has me fighting back the need to flip her over and take what I want.

She doesn't hesitate though. Whatever nerves she was fighting last night have vanished, replaced by the same passion she gets in the office.

"I want you to make me come. And then I want you to make me coffee." Her demanding tone is hot. She knows what she wants and it's sexy as hell.

If I weren't already hard as a rock, I would be now.

"Greedy little thing." I nip her ear a little harder this time before rolling her over and moving on top of her. "Do you have any idea how hot you look in my clothes, love?"

Val gives me a tiny smirk before cupping my dick over my pants. "Probably not as hot as you, but I bet we could even the playing field if we both took them off."

It takes me about two seconds to strip down and another two to strip her down. When we're both naked, I sit up, straddling her. I let my eyes get their fill of her body, snap-shotting every moment into my brain.

She's fucking perfect.

My hands cup her tits again as I lean down and kiss her. Every brush of my lips is a promise.

I'll take care of you. Kiss.

I'll make your coffee every morning. Kiss.

I'll have you seeing stars. Kiss.

I breathe in the taste of her, letting it drive me even more wild.

"More, please." The words aren't hard to make out, but they've barely left her mouth before she's back to kissing me.

Giving her one last kiss, I pull away from her mouth with a bite to her bottom lip, earning me a moan.

"I'm going to need more of those noises." I tell her this as I drag my mouth to her nipple. She squirms as I make contact, her hand coming to the back of my head to lock me in place.

I pull the hard little nub between my teeth and then

release it, running my tongue over it to provide a little relief. Then I do the whole process over.

My mouth begins searching for the other side, showing it just as much attention. I'm a fair guy that way.

"Can I taste you now, love?" I'm already moving down, leaving bites and kisses as I go.

"Fuck yes." As soon as the words leave her mouth, I'm at her center.

Pushing her legs open, I get a good look at my new favorite morning meal. "Look at this pretty little pussy. I can see you're wet for me."

I dive in. That's the only way to explain the animalistic way I begin to eat her out. Thrusting my tongue inside her, I make sure her entrance is slick enough before inserting a finger.

Val doesn't let me down, making sure I know just how much she's enjoying herself. She cries out and I hope like hell the other two can hear her.

"Yes, Romeo. Oh my god, more."

Let them hear how she's losing it for me, how she wants this.

With two fingers inside her, my mouth moves up to her clit. I suck it between my teeth and flick my tongue over and over.

"Yes. Please, Romeo. I'm almost here."

Watching Val get to the edge is fucking beautiful, but my girl wants to let go.

"You sound so sweet when you're begging me. You want to come, love? Come on my face for me. Like the greedy girl you are, ride my face."

Note to self, Val loves dirty talk. A gush of wetness hits my fingers and I curl them inside her as my mouth continues to wreak havoc on her clit.

"Holy fuck. Yes, yes, yes." Val gets louder and louder as

she comes for me, holding my face to her like she wants me to be permanently attached. I wouldn't object.

My fingers and my face are covered in her taste, but I don't stop until she's shaking with the aftershocks of her orgasm.

"Orgasm, check. Next up, coffee." I give her a kiss that she doesn't hesitate to return.

"Or I could show you how good I look on my knees in that fancy shower of yours." Her eyebrows wiggle up and down.

I know how much she likes her caffeine, but if she wants to suck my dick before she gets her fix, then I feel pretty damn special.

"Deal, but I'll probably lick that pussy again once you've swallowed my come."

Val's pushing me off her and running to my bathroom before I've finished my sentence.

Absolutely perfect.

Chapter Ten

Hart

I watch Romeo slowly feed Val strawberries while Beau makes her a second cup of coffee. I can't help but think how comfortable she looks in our home. She looks happy and well rested.

It's late in the morning and I know Beau will be claiming his nap time soon enough. Romeo hasn't stopped touching Val since we walked into the house last night. I'm not sure how he will react knowing his time with her is over.

We all heard the noises coming from Romeo's room this morning.

The strange thing is that I don't feel jealousy. I am ready for it to be my turn with her and I'm counting down the minutes.

And it should be weird watching my two best friends fawn over her but instead I just feel happy with how content they look. I've never felt so curious before. This dynamic isn't nearly as odd as it should be.

The three of them finish their breakfast and I watch Beau cleanup the dishes giving Romeo just a little more time with Val. As he finishes up the task, he walks over to me and quietly asks, "Do you think it would be okay if Val and I watched a movie and took a nap in the living room this afternoon?"

I shake my head. "I don't think that would be a problem. Are you wanting us to make ourselves scarce?"

He studies me quietly for a moment. "Actually, this might be weird, but I kind of enjoy adding her to our normal routine. Maybe give me a little bit of alone time to get to know her a little more." A smile takes over his face. "But I wouldn't mind if you both wanted to hang out with us for a while as well."

Beau knows I like being able to keep an eye on her and I'm guessing he's noticed how much Romeo wants to be touching her too. I appreciate that he's willing to share his time to accommodate that for us. So I just nod in thanks.

I've spent the last couple of hours in my room, trying to give Beau and Val some privacy. Tonight is my time with her and I'm not sure what I want to do with it. As much as I want her in my bed, I don't want her to think that's all I'm expecting.

Grabbing my phone, I decide to order groceries for the night. We have a grill on the patio along with outdoor heaters and it would be a great place for the four of us to have dinner.

Once the steaks and vegetables have been dropped off by the delivery service, I grab them from the front door and start setting up everything I'll need to prep dinner. Something about the idea of taking care of Val brings warmth to my chest. I can understand why Beau has been overly attentive with her, making sure she always has something to drink or snack on.

Beau and Val woke from their nap not too long ago. They spent some time together alone, as he requested, but Romeo joined them to watch a movie. The three of them are still in the living area so I don't have to raise my voice too loud to get their attention.

"Dinner should be ready soon enough, I thought we could eat on the patio. Romeo, would you mind turning on the heaters while I start the grill?"

He jumps up and grabs one of the trays from my hands before opening the sliding door to get to the patio.

When I came out to season the steaks, Beau and Val were cuddled up and sleeping on one section of the couch while Romeo was reading on another. Well, pretending to read. His eyes were more focused on Val than the upside-down dictionary he must have found lying around.

Beau winks at me, thanking me for giving him and Val a few more minutes to themselves. "Hope you like steak, my little danish. Hart is an expert meat handler."

Asshole.

I'm almost outside now, but I can still hear Val laughing. "Sounds like we have something in common then." There's no stopping the round of laughs she earns for that one.

I start throwing things on the grill, carefully keeping an eye on each item. Beau and Val come out with items to set the table.

"Any requests for how you'd like your steak cooked, darling?" The endearment leaves my lips before I can stop it, but it doesn't feel awkward. I still turn my eyes back to the food because I don't think I could handle seeing her reaction.

Val walks over and wraps her arms around my waist. A move I'm sure she isn't certain of but does so anyway to offer me some reassurance. "Medium for me please." Her voice is muffled against my back.

One of my hands uses tongs to begin flipping items over, the other hand grips her to me for another minute. We all have the same preference, so it shouldn't be too much longer before we're ready to eat.

When I let go, she does too. Despite the warmth of the patio, having her walk away from me feels cold. I could go grab the plates myself, but I'd much rather have her back over here with me.

"Hey, Val. Can you help me get everything plated?" She gives me a nod and together we have everyone served quickly. I shut off the grill and take my seat at the table.

While I'm seated at the head of the table, Beau is on my right. Romeo took a seat next to Val, and she's to my left. It's odd with how large the table is, but I like that we're all close.

Romeo opened up a bottle of wine for us all while I cooked, so we each have a full plate and a glass in front of us.

It feels like family.

My hand reaches out and squeezes Val's knee, only to graze across Romeo's on her other one. She looks up at me nervously, but I give her another squeeze and a small smile. I watch as she visibly relaxes before moving my hand away to cut into my food.

It's not long before an easy conversation picks up around the table. We all talk about where we are from, how we met. Val tells us about the small town she grew up in and how her best friend is constantly getting her into trouble.

Eventually, the topic turns to work, something that feels like an elephant in the room.

"Have you enjoyed working for Ground Up, snickerdoo-dle?" It amazes me that Beau keeps a straight face every time he drops one of his silly names for her.

She nods. "I have. It was my top choice after I finished the graduate program. I felt like it was a company that I could learn at but could also grow within."

"Of course, we could see how smart and driven you were the day of your interview." Romeo adds seriously. "It's why we hired you. I'm sure it's not just me that also finds those qualities extremely attractive either."

Beau is nodding in agreement and I find myself doing the same.

Val takes a bite of her steak and chews slowly, like she's giving herself time to think about what she wants to say next. "I was surprised to get the job, if I'm honest."

I set my utensils down. The other two don't seem to notice, but I can see that this is going somewhere serious. Val knows her worth as an individual and as an employee so there's not a chance her comment is fishing for praise. "Why do you say that, darling?"

We may be talking about work, but I want to remind her that right now we aren't just her bosses.

"I'm a woman." She gives nothing away with her tone or her body language and I'm unable to read what she means by that.

Beau seems confused, his eyebrows scrunched in on his forehead. "We hire plenty of women."

Her glass is steady in her hand as she brings it to her mouth, slowly sipping the liquid. I watch it travel down her throat, mesmerized by the way she swallows.

Later. Think of swallowing later. When we're alone.

"Sure. There are plenty of women in administrative roles around the office. I'm one of only three women hired amongst the design, engineering, and field teams. Were you all aware of that?"

I'm not sure that Beau and Romeo are, but I am, so I nod. "I appreciate you making sure we are aware of that. Equality is important to our company. Trust me, we've seen other female applicants come in before, but this industry doesn't have enough women walking through the doors to see the numbers even out."

I don't want to upset her, but I want to be honest with her. "The few women applicants who do come in aren't always ready to work in the environments we create. Not every woman can get through the interview process, either."

She rolls her eyes at me and I want to spank her. "This better not be a line about how I'm not like other girls since I managed to get through the process."

My friends don't speak up. Either they think I'm handling the conversation fine, or they think I'm about to sink myself into a hole I can't climb out of.

"Not at all, Val. Sure, some women walk through those doors and are easily intimidated by the three of us." Another eye roll has me counting two spankings in my head. "Then there are the female applicants who come in overly confident with nothing on their resumes to speak for it. Whether or not it's their fault that they couldn't get an internship or previous job experience, when we start asking the hard questions they falter."

She nods. She knows it's not an easy interview to get through. We give many scenarios to test how each applicant will respond to teamwork in the office, conflicts in the field, and many other trials we face in this business.

Val looks sad, as if she failed womankind by not having more to bring to the table for this conversation. I don't like it.

"Listen, darling. You make a great point. Let's start by seeing if we can find you a reliable, diverse team for your first project. After that, we can work together to see if there are any university programs that have more female interest for these sorts of job roles."

I reach over and set a hand on her shoulder. "Thank you

for trusting us enough to have this conversation. While we are aware of it, it doesn't mean we can understand it as well as someone on the other side. It's not an overnight fix, but there has to be opportunities we've missed before."

Or maybe we need to create those opportunities.

Val seems to be okay with this response and our topics turn less serious. Before long, Beau and Romeo excuse themselves, taking the dishes with them.

They've left what is still in the wine bottle and our glasses with us. Grabbing them, I lead Val over to our patio furniture. It's not much, but it's a nice enough spot for us to hang out a little longer.

"I'm sorry I made dinner a little awkward with my feminism." Her voice is quiet. "Not that I'm sorry for saying anything, but it may not have been the best time."

I move the hair from her shoulder before kissing the spot. "You didn't. I want you to feel comfortable talking about anything with me. Difficult topics or just about your day. Tell me anything, anytime."

She sighs and leans into me. "Today has been amazing."

It makes me happy that she sounds relaxed. "Good. You deserve it. Even when you roll your eyes and make me want to redden that ass of yours."

Her body stills against me and I curse myself. Sure, I have certain preferences in the bedroom, but most people have kinks. If they say they don't they are either lying or haven't found them yet.

I don't want to make Val uncomfortable by coming on too strong. My hand reaches out for her chin, turning her to face me. "Are you okay, darling?"

"Why would you want to spank me, Hart?" I like the way she says my name. It sends a shot of desire straight to my dick.

"You rolled your eyes at me, twice."

Val looks me in the eyes, studying me, and I do the same to her.

Then I watch as the corner of her mouth twitches before settling into a pout. "Did I earn myself a punishment, sir?"

Fuck. Damn. Holy shit. All the blood in my body goes south. My darling likes to play the brat.

"Do you want one?"

Val stands up slowly, sitting her wine down, but keeping her eyes trained on me. Then she bends over, gripping the back of the couch we're on. "Please."

I groan before standing up and moving behind her. My hands wander from her thighs upwards until I'm gripping her ass cheeks.

Val moans and squirms. I give her a light tap against her ass and she lets out a small whine. "You want more? You want me to turn that ass red?"

Her head nods, but it isn't enough. "Tell me with words, Val."

I watch her head turn until she makes eye contact with me. "Yes, sir."

My control slips away. I pull the sweatpants that are definitely too big for her down to her ankles. Fuck me, no underwear. Just her bare ass in front of me.

Fortunately, our patio is covered, and I doubt anyone could see us. Not that Val seems to mind. I think she might be a little exhibitionist.

Sliding my hand inside her thighs, I run a finger over her center. When it comes away glistening, I grunt, before bringing it to my mouth for a taste. "This for me, Val? Did you get wet thinking about your punishment? Or by the thought of someone catching us?"

When she doesn't answer me right away, I grab her by the neck, forcing her back against my chest. "Answer me, or I'll spank that ass so hard you'll be dripping, but I won't let you come."

"Both. I'm drenched because I want you to spank me and I wouldn't mind getting caught."

I push her back down, letting her assume her previous position. "Good girl."

Without warning, my hand smacks down on her ass, the sound ringing out into the dark. She flinches away, but wiggles back towards me for more.

"I think four more, then I'm going to bury myself so deep inside you that you'll feel empty for days when I'm done."

One. Two. Three. Four.

Each one has her letting out a noise. A moan, a whine, a mewl. Each time she wants more.

When I'm done, I slide my fingers into her. "Your cunt is dripping for me, dirty girl. You want to come for me?"

"Yes!" She yells loudly and I use my other hand to cover her mouth and pull her back to me.

"When we're inside, be as loud as you want, darling. Right now, I need you to be quiet for me. Shout into my hand as I fuck you with my fingers, alright?"

She nods and I start up again. Fingering her tight little hole from behind until she's writhing and shaking, falling over the edge.

"I want to sink inside you right here, but not tonight." I lift her into my arms, her borrowed sweatpants forgotten on the ground.

As I carry her into my room, she clings on to me. I don't see Beau or Romeo, and right now I don't care.

I slam the door closed with my foot before tossing her onto my bed. "Take that shirt off for me, darling."

She does so and I tear off my own clothes. I throw out another order as I walk over to my nightstand and grab a condom. "Lay at the edge, your legs off the bed, face down."

Val doesn't hesitate to take up the position and I'm rolling the rubber over my length just as fast.

"This is going to be hard and probably fast, babe. I'll make it up to you in round two."

"Don't care. Get inside me, please." Her voice is muffled by the bed, her face pressed against the mattress.

"I'd spank you for making demands, but you added that please. You sound sexy when you're needy for me." I mean it. I like her begging.

Standing behind her, I push in slowly. She's wet, but I don't want to take any chances of hurting her.

One hand on her hip, the other in her hair, I go wild. Thrusting hard over and over again. "Let me hear you now, dirty girl."

"So good. You fuck me so good, Hart." My name on her lips has me rutting into her like an animal.

"Harder, please. Oh, yes. Yes." Val's voice sounds far away now. I'm too far gone.

"That pretty little cunt takes my cock so good, baby." The praise has her clenching around me. "You going to come for me?"

She nods and I remove the hand from her hair to snake around and circle her clit. "Now. Come for me, right now."

Val shatters and I'm right behind her. I push inside her as deep as I can go and she moves against me trying to pull me in. I'm not sure how much time passes before I pull out of her and she whines when she's empty.

"Don't worry, darling. Let's clean up so we can do it again."

I keep my word as I let her ride my face and then my dick again before we both pass out, completely spent.

Chapter Eleven

Beau

I've been looking forward to this afternoon for hours. I heard the noises coming from Romeo's room yesterday morning and then again from Hart's room last night.

And I want to earn some noises of my own.

So today, instead of lounging in the living area, I've decided to take Val to my room. We had breakfast and lunch with the other guys, but I've finally got her to myself. She is lying beside me as we face each other.

My hand is playing with her hair as she smiles at me. It's a moment in time I could freeze frame and spend every day replaying. We've been laying for probably an hour, playing twenty questions.

Some about ourselves, some inappropriate, some completely random.

"Tell me a dream, cookie cake."

"Any dream?" She asks sleepily.

"Any dream you're willing to share with me." I confirm.

She's silent for a while and I start to think she's fallen asleep. "I think I'd like to start a program for young girls. I know there are a lot out there nowadays for science and engineering, but I think there should be more. Not interior design either. For everything that it takes to start, build, and complete a project."

The passion in her voice is making me hard and Val can tell. "If anyone could do it, it'd be you, Val. One day. Let me be a part of it though, deal?"

"Deal."

I listen to her breathing even out as she falls asleep in my arms. She had a long, hard day yesterday. At least that is what I'm guessing from the times I've peeked on Romeo and Hart in the bathroom over the years. I'm pretty sure they're packing satisfactory bedroom skills.

As I fall asleep, I try to think of the perfect way to wake my little pie crust later.

—-

It's warm in this bed. Too warm and almost uncomfortable. When I open my eyes, it's clear what the problem is.

Val is still curled up beside me, but behind her is another body. A body that's wrapped around her like a koala bear. She doesn't seem to mind being squished between us, and I'm not really upset with him for joining us, but it's not exactly cool.

"Romeo!" I whisper yell at him. I was planning to wake up Val with my face between her thighs. "You're interrupting my nap time."

He peeks at me with one eye open. Fucker, he's not even sleeping, just curled up around our girl like she's his oxygen source. "Sorry."

There's not an ounce of sincerity in that apology. He's ruining my plans and I am not missing a chance to taste my tootsie roll.

"I wanted to lick Val's pussy until she woke up, so you've got to go." I make a shoo motion with my hands.

Val chooses that moment to open her eyes. "What is

going on? Oh, Romeo." She stretches out between us. "I thought I felt you climb in bed, but I thought it was a dream. I'm guessing the threesome was a dream though. Shame."

She's so casual with her words. Like she didn't offer up the holy grail of fantasies. Not just a threesome, but her.

Romeo and I stay silent, our eyes catching on one another. We've never done that. In all our years, the three of us have never even slept with the same woman, let alone shared one.

I smile. "You want us both, sugar lips?"

She narrows her eyes, trying to determine if I'm serious. "Don't tease me."

"Never, Val." I use her name so she knows just how serious I am. Lowering my mouth to hers, I kiss her deeply. "Any specific requests? We've never done this, so we'll have to wing it."

"In my experience, a threesome without a plan is the best kind." There's no joke in her tone. Fuck.

Romeo's eyes light with jealousy, but I shake my head. We've all got a past.

"Alright then. I'm still licking that pussy, though. You want to sit on my face, darling?" I roll on to my back. "Romeo, strip her."

He moves fast, getting her naked in record time. I'm pretty sure I heard threads ripping, but I don't give a shit.

"Sit on his face, love. Then I'll let you choke on my dick."

Val moves immediately, straddling my face and hovering over me. Not acceptable. I pull her down until I'm struggling to breathe. Perfect.

I plan on drowning in her, so I get to work. My tongue circles her clit and then snakes down to thrust into her. I repeat this pattern a couple of times while finding the right rhythm to have Val grinding against me.

With this position, I can't see what the other two are doing, but I can hear them.

The sound of Romeo's groans and Val's mouth working him over. It's really fucking hot.

I grab on to her hips and encourage to take what she wants. She moans and the taste of her fills my mouth. I'm imagining Romeo's hands pulling at her sweet little nipples while she pulls him deep into her mouth.

"Stop now, love. I want to come down your throat while you ride Beau's dick." Romeo's weight leaves the bed and I hear the sound of my drawer opening and closing.

Val speeds up, soaking my mouth and chin, until the sound of her grabbing my headboard and coming undone fills the room.

I wonder if she'll let me record the noise and set it as her ringtone. Probably not.

Her weight is removed from my face and I see Romeo lifting her up and over my very hard dick. He hands her a condom. "Put it on him and then climb on."

He looks at me and smirks. "Sorry about this but try and keep your eyes on her tits. They are phenomenal."

My confusion clears up when he steps over my head. His ass is sitting against my headboard while his feet are on either side of my neck. I can see his nuts, swinging above me like a testicle pendulum of doom.

It bothers me for all of one minute before Val is rolling the condom on me and then sliding me inside her wet pussy.

"Oh fuck. You're so wet. Yes, ride me. Hard." It feels amazing having her on top of me, taking whatever she wants to chase her own needs.

Romeo's hand reaches out and pulls her mouth down on him again. "Good girl. You want to fuck Beau while I fuck your mouth?"

She moans. Sweet Jesus this woman is fucking perfect.

My thumb goes to her clit, circling faster and faster. Val rides me harder and harder, bobbing against Romeo's length.

It's the most beautiful sight I've ever seen. Romeo grunts, holding her head in place as he comes in her mouth and I watch her lick him up.

He and his dick move out of my view as Val starts to work overtime on me.

"You feel so good, Beau." She gives praise as good as she takes it.

Romeo moves behind her, his fingers working with mine against her clit. Val begins to shake between us, falling against my chest.

If it bothers him that he's pretty close to touching my dick, he doesn't show it. Instead, he gathers the wetness he finds before slipping around and inserting a finger in her ass.

Val shatters. Her body shakes and she screams, clenching so tight around me that I come hard too.

Romeo and I are wearing matching smug smiles. He grabs Val off of me. "Come on, love. Let's show Beau how much you like to use the shower to get dirty."

He tosses her over his shoulder, smacking her ass, while I roll off the bed and dispose of the condom.

As I follow the other two to my bathroom, I see that my bedroom door is cracked open. Which is interesting, since it was definitely closed when things got started and there's only one other person in the house who could have peeked inside.

Chapter Twelve

Val

The weekend is slowly coming to an end and I'm not any closer to making a decision. It doesn't feel right to pick one because I'm so happy with all of them.

Beau is cheesy as hell, but cute and considerate. He makes sure not only I've eaten, but that both of his friends are taken care of too.

Romeo has one of the filthiest mouths in the bedroom. Outside of the bedroom, he's affectionate and sweet as can be. If I'm close to him, he's finding a way to touch me.

Hart is controlling and bossy, but my mind feels safe with him. If I just turn it off, he'll take care of me. The way he watches me like he can see my thoughts is unnerving and exciting.

If I'm honest with myself, when I woke up from my nap earlier, it didn't feel awkward at all. Cuddled up between Beau and Romeo felt almost perfect. I just wish Hart had been there. Maybe there's a configuration where I could still touch all of them while I sleep.

I'm feeling the effects of back-to-back sex, exhausted and

in need of a warm bath for my lady bits, but I feel...more than happy. I'm not sure what to call this feeling, but I like it.

We're sitting at the dining table finishing dinner but it's quieter than this house has been since the moment I first walked in. Like we are all dreading what happens next. Even with the dark cloud hovering over the table, this feels so easy.

I stand from the table and take my plate to the sink. They've catered to my every comfort all weekend, but my skin is itching with the need to get up and away. I start to collect the guy's plates as well, even though they protest.

"I'm going to go change and call an Uber." I've spent the last two days in their clothes. Covered in their scents and comfort. I'm currently wearing one of Beau's band shirts with a pair of Romeo's boxers. The guys are in their sweatpants, differing colors of gray. It's very distracting.

"Why?" Beau sounds genuinely confused.

I snort. "It's Sunday. I have to get ready for work tomorrow. You know, that whole job thing you guys pay me for?"

Romeo chuckles. "I've never hated a Monday more."

That cloud comes over us again.

"Well, if you must leave, then let us give you a proper goodbye." Hart's voice draws my attention.

"Please tell me what your idea of proper is, Hart." I roll my eyes.

He's up and standing in front of me faster than I can exhale.

"Now, baby girl. Don't roll your eyes at me. I'd hate to have to punish you when I really want to worship you with my best friends."

Oh shit. I can't even stop myself. "I'd rather have both, please."

He growls and reaches out his hand to run over my

throat. His grip closes over it and he drags me forward until our mouths are just barely touching. "If you insist."

Even though Hart is smiling, it's sinister. I'm already soaked.

He pushes me back to the table by the grip on my throat before spinning me around. His hands come up to my hips and he begins lifting up my shirt. "Look at them."

Romeo and Beau are frozen in their chairs with lust filled eyes watching every movement. Romeo's hands are clenched on his thighs, but Beau is clearly onboard with this plan. He's got one hand down his sweats touching himself.

I let out a moan at the sight and Beau quickly stands to push down the pants. Sitting back down naked, he continues to stroke himself.

"You're so fucking beautiful, Val. No wonder we all want you. Need you." Hart has one hand traveling down and the other pulling at my nipples. When the other hand reaches its destination, he groans. "You want us too. This needy little cunt is drenched thinking about taking us all."

"Not all at once. I'm up for just about anything, but triple penetration seems like something you work up to. I bet I could do double though." I have no idea what the hell I'm saying. I'm nervous, but he's right. I want them all.

The guys have frozen at my blubbering. "Oh, please don't stop. We can totally wing it. Continue."

I can feel Hart smile against the crook of my neck, but he bites down and I let out a small scream as my legs buckle. He chuckles as he catches me.

"You said you wanted punishment, baby girl. Lay against the table and watch them. Don't come or I'll spank you." He drops to his knees behind me as I obey.

My eyes lock with Romeo's and I watch his resistance snap. He stands and removes his own clothing just as Hart's fingers sink into me.

"I'm going to eat this pussy until you're on the edge. Be a good girl and we will give you what you want, but if you come, I'm going to spank you then we'll take turns fucking your face and you'll miss out on what you're craving."

I clench around his fingers at the word *spank* and he bites one of my ass cheeks. There's no chance to respond to the threat because his tongue is rimming my ass before moving to meet his fingers.

Fingers he replaces with his tongue. Hart is fucking me with his face, smothering himself with me. My hands grip the edges of the table as I squirm. It's erotic and overwhelming. He's trying to become a part of me while his friends watch on.

"Hold on, sweetie. You're doing so good." Romeo speaks up and I break eye contact, squeezing them shut. "No. Watch us. Look at Beau or me, but you give us your eyes."

I nod in agreement, this time moving my eyes to Beau. His hand is gripping his cock hard and I smile. I feel Hart reposition himself shortly before his fingers are thrusting back into me and he bites my clit.

"No, no, no." I'm shaking my head back and forth fighting the pleasure coursing through me. The table barely moves even as I hold on and thrash. I hold my breath until the feeling passes. I did it. I didn't come.

"You're so perfect for us, baby girl. Good job." I soak up Hart's praise as he stands and lifts me off the table. He puts us face to face before rubbing his thumb over my bottom lip. I open for him and he grins, shoving two fingers in my mouth. I suck every bit of me from his skin before biting down.

He laughs. "Give Romeo a taste."

Romeo is already standing beside us and he grabs my face with both hands, devouring my mouth. His tongue is searching out any taste he can get. He pulls me out of Hart's arms and into his own, picking me up and wrapping my legs around him as he starts walking.

He continues kissing me. His teeth latch on to my bottom lip as he sits us down on that couch. "We're all clean." His hands are stroking my face with a gentleness as he says it. Romeo's eyes are soft and serious. All of the actions together feel very…loving.

"Me too. I have an implant in my arm, too." I tell him as I grind my wetness against his bare length. The noise should embarrass me, but I'm lost to this. To them. To us.

"Wasn't even thinking about it, but good. I want to slide into you and feel this dripping pussy on my dick. I want to fuck you hard and fill you up, love." He lays back on the couch, positioning me over him.

I'm so fucking happy for their giant couch right now. No part of me is hanging off, making it easy to straddle him and sink down.

"Holy shit. Oh fuck. That's Heaven." Romeo lets me take my time sliding down until he's all the way in. "Sweet, sweet girl. I'm going to need you to be still. I'm dying right now and this is the way to fucking go. My dick drowning in your soaking wet heat. Lord take me out now, it's never getting better than this."

I laugh at his ridiculous ramble. There's the sound of footsteps and I hear a door open and close. Did the other two leave us?

"Not that I don't think you could rock my world until we both black out, but I thought I was promised a triple whammy after that torture?"

The other two join us laughing. "Sorry, sugar pie. Had to go grab something."

Beau holds up a bottle of lube and I'm nodding in consent as fast as I can.

"Let me give you a distraction while Romeo keeps dying

under you and Beau preps you." Hart is standing at the end of the couch with his very naked dick right in front of me. My mouth is searching him out right away, but he steps back. "Nu-uh, baby girl. I'll give it to you when I want to."

Romeo groans. "She really likes that whole bossy thing you have going on. Her pussy just gushed around me."

Hart kisses me slowly, his hand seeking out both nipples. He starts sweet, feeling them up, and then he's pulling at them again.

I really, really like when they play with my nipples. The whining noise I make confirms that.

Beau's lips are kissing my shoulder and back, soft and sweet. His hands are trailing down my sides and over my ribcage drawing out a shiver.

I'm barely rocking on Romeo as I feel a finger at my ass. It slides in easy enough with the lube, but when Beau pulls out to add another I tense.

His kisses start up again. "It's okay. We'll take care of you, Val. I promise."

That sounds like more of a beginning than a goodbye, but I know I'm reading too much into it.

Beau's fingers continue to loosen me up as he scissors them inside of me. It feels so good that I'm squirming on top of Romeo who's got a death grip on my hips trying to keep me still.

Hart keeps kissing me sweetly unlike the pinch he just gave both my nipples. "You're going to look so good all filled up, baby girl. Beau is going to fuck that ass while Romeo takes you. And if you let them do that, I'll let you suck my dick."

I nod. I want that. I want to see Hart lose his mind when I deep throat him down.

Beau starts pushing inside of me slowly. Relaxing my body, I focus on their voices.

Telling me I'm beautiful. That I'm made to take them all. That I'm perfect.

They make me believe it.

Once Beau is fully seated, I can't stay still anymore. "Please. I need you." My voice is soft.

Hart kisses me on the mouth again as his friends start to move.

"Oh, fuck. That's so tight." Beau's groaning as he starts slow.

Romeo loses his control and starts thrusting upwards hard.

I start grinding back and forth causing a series of curses.

"Give me that mouth, baby" Hart finally lets me have him and I don't hesitate to swallow him down. "Oh shit. Never going to last if you do that."

Hollowing out my cheeks, I look up into his eyes. He smiles and softly slaps my cheek, making me moan. "You want me to fuck your face, baby girl?"

I pull back and smile. He gathers my hair, wrapping it around his hand. "Put me back in your mouth."

I open wide and he thrusts forward, choking me. "That's it. Take me down. Take all three of us in all your hot little holes."

We all start moving faster together. My nails dig into Romeo's chest.

"Come. I want to see you come while you choke me down." Hart pulls my hair as he makes his demand, but I'm not the only one he orders around. "No one else. Just Val."

Beau and Romeo cuss at him, but Romeo puts his fingers around my clit and squeezes just as Hart pulls my head back. I detonate, screaming loud. It seems to go on forever. My vision blacks out.

When I come back to Earth, everyone has paused their

actions. I know they're all staring at me, even though I'm barely conscious.

"Are you okay, honey bun?" Beau is rubbing a hand up and down my back. Romeo is kissing my chest.

Hart lifts my face. "Words, Val. We lost you there for a second."

"I'm okay. Just left my body."

They laugh but don't move.

"More. I need all of you to come too. Together, please."

Eyes still locked on mine, Hart's face is blank. When I nod, he nods back. "Okay."

Romeo starts slowly, but Beau's the one who snaps this time. He starts pounding, one hand on my shoulder, the other squeezing an ass cheek. Romeo's carefulness doesn't last long. Soon they are both fucking me hard and fast.

I open my mouth for Hart, wanting him back. He chuckles and moves to accommodate my request.

Soon he's back to drilling into my lips with force. Losing control looks beautiful on him. "I'm about to come, baby girl."

Beau and Romeo both say something similar and soon they're all grunting and chasing their release.

Hart brings my head all the way to the end of his length as he releases. He holds me there for several seconds, making sure every drop is out. "That's a really good girl. Swallow me down. All of it."

When he's down, he hooks his thumb in my mouth and pulls until he can examine it. There's nothing there to see. I drank down every bit.

He smiles and kisses me deeply before stepping back. When he does, I look down to Romeo. The jealousy from before seems to have burned away. I'm sure it's under the surface, but it's been replaced with a look of adoration.

"I want my eyes locked on yours when I lose myself, gorgeous. Can you do that?"

I adjust myself until one hand is holding my weight on one side of his head and the other is on his chest, moving towards his cheek.

It's an intimate moment, but Romeo's pace is brutal. It feels amazing and I'm getting close to the edge again.

Romeo thrusts up and holds himself there, spilling inside me. He doesn't break his eye contact until he relaxes beneath me. Even then, it's just so he can stretch up to kiss me. He pulls out of me and there's a mess that follows. He doesn't seem to care about that or the fact that I probably still taste like his friend.

Then he puts his hands behind his head and grins. "Perfect. You're perfect."

I can't help but grin back.

Beau grabs one of my arms, lifting me to his chest. "Still here, babe."

A normal pet name. I didn't know he had it in him. "Dude, you're in my ass. Kind of hard to forget about that." I clench around him just to be a little bratty.

He grunts. "Fuck."

Soon, he's drilling into me at an impossible pace. "Such a tight ass."

I lose myself to his movements. Reaching an arm back to wrap around his head. His mouth comes down on my neck.

Beau kisses me gently before addressing his friends. "I bet our greedy girl wants to come again."

It'll probably kill me, but yeah, I do.

I've barely blinked before they are all back to surrounding me. Romeo thrusts two fingers into me, and then adds a third. My eyes widen at the sensation. He's curling them into the mess of both of us and it's so full with Beau behind me.

Hart's at my side, running a hand down and slapping my pussy repeatedly in quick succession.

Beau bites down on my neck and pulls out to come on my ass.

As soon as those teeth break my skin, I'm tumbling into the darkness.

I have two thoughts as I pass out.

One, they are going to have to get this couch professionally cleaned. Two, I'll never have another sexual encounter to live up to this moment as long as I live.

Chapter Thirteen

Beau

After Val passed out on us, she only took a small nap before insisting she went home for the night.

I'm sure it was a lot. Not just the whole blacking out twice from coming so hard, but the last forty-eight hours included. It was one of the highlights of my life and I know that Romeo and Hart are in agreement.

We made sure she was safely in the Uber, Hart demanding that she send over the driver's details to us in a group text, and the three of us came out to our heated patio for a drink.

"She's it. I'm telling you right now, I'm going to marry that woman." Romeo likes to pretend he's not a hopeless romantic, but the dude grew up with parents who instilled their belief of soulmates into him deeply.

I get it. We've all had serious relationships, dated and fucked around.

This weekend was different. Val is different.

My sugar blossom has us all in a tiff.

Hart hasn't spoken, but ever since he started the group

activity scene earlier, there's been a determination in his eyes.

"What is it, you broody asshole?" I ask.

He huffs out a breath and sits back in his chair. "I watched you both with her this weekend. Your feelings are very clear. I won't deny that my own are very strong."

Romeo's fists are clenching.

"Hear me out." Hart has his business voice turned up. The one he uses with asshole clients who try to take advantage of how small our firm is by asking for lower bids on their projects. He hates that.

I cross my arms over my chest, not sure where he's taking this. I fucking hope we're on the same page.

"What if she doesn't choose?"

I smile. "Spell it all the way out, lover boy. I'm pretty sure I'm in, but Romeo is going to need all the bullet points."

Hart grins at me. That's my buddy. My pal.

"We all care about her. Clearly, none of us want to walk away from her. I think we proved tonight that we make a good team, and not just at the office."

That gets a chuckle from all three of us.

Romeo runs his hand over his head. "You want to…share her?"

I'm nodding. "Yupp, I'm in. I like Val and I love the two of you. I'd never want to see any of you hurt, but I can't see myself walking away from her either."

"It's up to her, of course. I just don't see why we can't continue with what we had this weekend. We all had plenty of alone time with her, even if we all wanted more, but she fits into this dynamic so easily. If you really think about it, with how crazy all of our schedules are and the different hours we work when we are deep into a project, it makes plenty of sense to enter into a group relationship."

Hart adds in that last part for himself, but he's right. One of us alone would try to make as much time for Val as they could and it wouldn't be enough. Not like she deserves. The three of us together could make sure she's always safe and cared for.

And fucked. A lot. I need a million repeats of tonight's sexcapades.

I look at Romeo. "What do you think?"

He sighs. "I think I'm going to end up sharing my future wife with you two assholes."

Hell yes.

——

The next morning, we are all waiting for Val, watching her desk on the security cameras. Hart sent an appointment to her calendar to meet us in his office.

We watch as she comes in and sets her things down before logging into her computer and presumably checking her email.

A frown comes over her face. I hate it.

Val sits there for another minute before standing up and heading to the elevator. As soon as we see this, Hart turns off the camera view and we all attempt to look casual.

Another few minutes pass before Val is knocking on the door. I'm the closest so I get to let her in.

"Good morning, cheesecake." The silly name gets a small smile out of her. Much better than a frown. "Come sit with us."

Romeo has a cup of coffee in his hand that he gives her. "Morning, love." He kisses her cheek before standing over to the side.

I take the open chair next to Val while Hart stays seated at his desk.

"We'd like to talk about the decision we asked you to make." He sounds so formal. As if we didn't all spend the weekend inside her.

She nods. "I assumed."

My hand is already moving to her knee. Romeo eyes it like he wants to cut it off. He's been trying to touch her any chance he can and I'm betting the only reason he doesn't have her in his lap is because he's nervous about her reaction.

"Clearly, we all enjoyed ourselves this weekend. You're an intelligent and beautiful woman." Hart's phrasing sounds like a breakup and Val must sense the same because she flinches under my hand.

I'm going to have to take the lead this time around. "What he means is, we talked after you left last night and we all want to continue to see you."

Her face scrunches up in confusion. "Like another weekend?"

Romeo nods. "Yes, like this weekend. Except more of a long-term deal."

"We've spoken and we think it could work." Hart adds.

Val nods, too. She speaks business just like Hart, so I decide to pitch out some of his points from last night.

"Listen, we're busy people. With the new project coming up, it's only going to get busier. It makes sense that we all continue to see you when we can." For a guy not so great at the fancy words, I think I'm doing pretty good.

She looks to Romeo and Hart, but both are in agreement.

"You want to fuck me when it's convenient because all of our lives are busy? Just keep a schedule like we did all weekend?" She asks, her voice clear and strong.

"Exactly." She's in. I just know it. We've got her.

"With all due respect, fuck off. I am not a toy to be used when you have some extra time and want to pencil me into your calendar."

Or I'm wrong.

"No, Val. That isn't-" We all try to get a word in, but she interrupts us.

"I will not be okay being your fuck toy. This weekend meant something to me. I've been beating myself up since I left yesterday trying to figure out what I was going to do. I care about all of you, but it was just about sex for you? Bullshit." She stands and straightens out her outfit, her shoulders pushed back in defiance.

"Consider this weekend a mistake. In fact, it never happened. I'm still the same employee from last week and none of you have ever seen me naked."

We're all still standing in shock as she exits the office, never looking back.

Chapter Fourteen

Val

S tumbling into the bathroom, I head for the first stall and slam it closed behind me. I pull out my phone and dial Noel.

"Please tell me you're calling me after being freshly fucked in some ridiculous boardroom. I need every detail, leave nothing out."

When I got home last night, Noel made her stance on Team Harem very clear. She even took the time to draw several diagrams of group sex positions that had to defy gravity and anatomy.

I sniffle.

"Oh no. What happened, babe? I know a guy who knows a girl who fucked an inmate one time. I bet they have connections. Is the hit on all three of them? Or just one? You know what, don't tell me now. My government agent is probably listening. I'll work out a code and explain it when you get home."

My voice cracks and I sob into the phone. "I didn't give them the chance to fuck me. They called me up to Hart's office as soon as I came in this morning. They said they wanted to make me theirs. It caught me off guard because I thought they were going to tell me to pick. At first, they were all romantic and saying sweet things, but then they started talking about how convenient it would be because of how busy they are. I was just going to be their exclusive booty call."

I really hope I'm alone here, because I start crying louder.

"What a bunch of dicks. They just want pussy on tap? I really thought after this weekend you were going to tell me you got a happily dicking after with all of them"

I don't respond and she hums.

"Val, I love and adore you. You know that, right?"

"Yeah, No-No. I know."

She takes a deep breath. "Good. Now pull your head out of your ass. I bet you didn't stick around long enough to really hear them out. There's no way they want to be fuck buddies only. This isn't the time to run scared. Damn it, it's time to jump. Jump on those glorious dicks and ride them into the sunset."

I laugh at the absurdity, but I know she's right. I ran because I was scared they didn't really want me.

"I have to go, Noel. I'll talk to you later."

Hanging up the phone, I walk out of the stall. The bathroom is empty, thankfully.

When I left their place last night, I felt lonely. I wanted to hear Beau's laugh, feel Romeo's hand on my knee, let Hart boss me around.

In a short time, I grew attached to them. Not just for the sex. Not that it wasn't absolutely perfect and hot and mind-blowing.

All of the little moments are what really weigh on me. Kisses on my cheek, bringing me a glass of water just because, having wine delivered to the house because I don't drink their favorite beer.

I felt spoiled and precious. It's an addicting thing and I'm terrified to chase it.

What happens when they grow tired of me? Maybe experimenting with a group relationship is a midlife crisis. I'll be the one left broken and alone while they move on together.

Or worse, what if their friendship is fractured by the pressure of sharing me?

What if I'm building this all up in my head and they don't have feelings as strong as mine?

I'll have to face the guys at some point, but it doesn't have to be today. I need some time to think.

I exit the building a half hour earlier than normal. I couldn't do it anymore. Sitting at my desk trying to focus on bundling the interior team for the project wasn't working. I'd look through the lists and get pissed off that there are barely any women included. Then I'd think about how I could bring it up to the guys.

Then I'd think about the guys. Their touches, the way we connected. The way they looked when I took off this morning.

I couldn't pretend I wasn't hurting. Noel's words have stayed with me all day. The guys tried to tell me what they wanted and I didn't listen.

Instead, I threw their words back at them assuming the worst. As if we didn't spend the entire weekend learning everything about each other, not just our bodies, but our souls too.

"Val."

My bullshit spiral comes to a halt as I take in the sight in front of me.

Beau. Hart. Romeo.

They're waiting in sleek black tuxedos, each man holding a different bouquet of flowers. The tears I've been holding back since my bathroom breakdown begin to flow.

"Fuck. Tears. I can't do the water works; I'm tagging one of you in." Romeo sounds frantic because I'm crying, but I know I could walk up to him now and he'd hold me through it.

Instead, Hart surprises me by wrapping his arms around me. Not because he's any less affectionate. No, he's living up to his name and his heart is bigger than all three of their giant dicks combined.

"Please take a drive with us, darling. Really hear us out this time. We fucked up this morning, but I know we can fix it."

My head has barely finished nodding before he's leading me into the limo. All three climb in behind me and it takes serious strength to not climb one or two of them immediately. I can be patient, though. I'm a grown ass woman.

Beau starts the conversation, but the car stays still. "First, I'm really sorry about this morning. I was excited and got really carried away."

I crinkle my brows. "You didn't mean you all wanted to be with me?"

"Fuck, Beau. Just be quiet for a minute." Romeo pats Beau's shoulder and squeezes. "His intentions are pure, but he's not putting all the thoughts into words well."

He leans forward and takes my hand. "Of course, we want to be with you. What we are trying to tell you is that this weekend was amazing. All of us want to give this relationship with you a chance. You are intelligent and kind. Beautiful and daring. Naughty and nice."

Romeo winks as Beau shoves him. "Wrong holiday, fucker."

Hart grabs my other hand. "We all have very strong feelings for you and none of us are willing to hurt the others by asking you to choose."

I gulp.

That sounds nice, but how do we make it work? "Are you all planning to date me together?"

Beau can't contain himself any longer and hops over to my side of the limo. "Yes. There will be times where we take you on individual dates, but we might have some group outings, too. Everything will be out in the open within our love nest."

"For fuck's sake." Romeo rolls his eyes, but he's smiling. "He's right though. We are all dedicated to this. All of us are busy, including you. All we meant by that was it was a pro to sharing you. Between the three of us, we could always be certain you were taken care of in the way you deserve. I'm sure there will be challenges and many, many benefits."

Orgasms. He definitely means orgasms.

"We want you, Val." Hart's voice is deep and authoritative, his statement sounding like a promise.

"I want you, too. All of you. This weekend was the best time of my life and I want more. I was hurting this morning. The thought of picking between you kept me up all night. I couldn't do it. I don't know what kind of future that will bring, but I'm in to give it a try." The words have barely left my mouth before I'm jumping into waiting arms.

Hart catches me and slams his mouth on mine. "Thank fuck."

I watch him press a button on the door and the car starts to move.

Romeo and Beau are kissing either side of my neck and shoulders as my arms reach out to hold them to me.

My clothes are slid off of me quickly as I start unbuttoning Hart's shirt. "Need you. Right now."

His groans break our kiss to look down at me grinding against his hardness. My panties are ripped off as he leans me backwards and into Romeo's lap behind me. Hart's pants are pushed down, but he doesn't enter me right away. Instead, he grabs my ass and brings my pussy to his mouth.

"Oh fuck." Hopefully the driver is being paid well for his discretion, because my guys like to make me scream.

My guys. I like the sound of that.

Hart shoves his tongue inside of me while Romeo leans down to capture my mouth.

"You're so fucking sexy, candy lips." Beau and his damn nicknames. He makes up for it by pulling a nipple with one hand and sucking the other into his mouth.

"More. I need more."

"You need my dick in your cunt? You need me so deep inside you that you can't breathe?" Hart sucks my clit into his mouth hard as he shoves two fingers into me.

Romeo swallows my moans down as he fucks my mouth with his tongue, but I pull away.

"Please, I need all of you." I'll leave the logistics up to them. I just want more.

Beau grabs my face with both hands. "You have us."

Hart roughly flips me over before entering me hard from behind. Grabbing my hair and pulling me up. Once I'm close enough, his hand wraps around my neck. "Use your hand on Beau and let Romeo fuck your mouth. I want to see you all lose it while I fuck this tight cunt."

Just as fast as he brought me up, he shoves me right back down. Romeo grabs my chin until I'm looking up at him. His left eyebrow raises to ask if this is okay and I nod my consent.

"Get it nice and wet for me, honey. I want it sliding in and out of your mouth without resistance. Otherwise, I might just put it down your throat and stay there while you gag until I come."

I mean, if you insist. I start with a kiss on the tip before dragging my tongue from his base and all the way up. It's not long before he's shoving his way past lips and into the back of my mouth.

Hart doesn't let me forget who's really in charge, though. His hands are gripping my hips hard.

I'll proudly wear every bruise and mark they give me because I am theirs.

Beau is gentler. He gives me time to find my rhythm and then he lifts one of my hands and runs his tongue over it. He wraps it around his length alongside his own hand until we are both jacking him off together.

They are all using me to chase pleasure, but I know I'll get triple the amount from them. It's not long before Hart's arm is wrapping around my waist to play with my clit again.

"Give it to us, Val. Now." I obey and see stars.

Romeo is grunting and fucking my mouth faster. "Another one."

This time Beau reaches his free arm under me to pull at a nipple. I'm almost there.

"Look at me. Give me your eyes as I fuck this gorgeous face." Romeo's gaze locks with mine and I shatter for them again. I'm not sure when I broke eye contact, but when I look up at him again his eyes are rolling back and he releases into my mouth.

I drink down every drop before removing my mouth with a pop. I don't hesitate to lean over and take Beau next.

"Oh baby, I'm already coming." He doesn't lie. I'm swallowing him down in seconds. He and Romeo lean down and kiss either side of my face. Then they lean back into their seats and watch as Hart loses it.

His thrusts are getting faster and faster. Harder and deeper. I look back and watch him. He squeezes my ass and throws his head back, coming hard inside of me.

It feels like it's been hours since we got into this limo. I don't know where we are headed, but I can say with certainty I'd go anywhere with them.

My valentines.

Except maybe The Golden Arrow. While the bow may have aimed true for me, Cupid is totally still a cunt.

The End

I hope you all enjoyed Val's story.
This isn't the last time we will see them, as Noel's
story is coming this winter.
Our favorite elf will be bringing the Christmas chaos
before you know it.

Acknowledgments

There are a few people I would like to thank. First, my family. My husband and mother-in-law who help with Rosie in order for me to sit down and write.

The trinity....I wrote you a dedication. That's all you're getting.

My PA, Nikki who takes care of so many things so that I can spend my free time writing! And designing this amazing cover.

My beta team. Rachel, thank you for hoping in to any words I send you without question. I adore you. Jess, you bring me so much joy with your messages. Heather, thanks for letting me harass you regularly.

And to my darlings and damsels, my readers...thank you for all the kind things you've said about my writing. I wouldn't ever sit at the keyboard if it weren't for you.

About the Author

Drea Denae lives in Texas with her family.

She believes strongly in ice coffee year round, wearing red lipstick whenever the hell she wants, and listening to Taylor Swift on repeat.

Use the QR code below to find Drea's other books and follow her on social media.

Printed in Great Britain
by Amazon

79210781R00059